Finding Happiness

Emma Blair

In Five Volumes

Volume One

RNIB supporting blind and partially sighted people

Published by Time Warner Books UK, London.

This Giant Print edition published 2011 by RNIB

ISBN 0 316 85872 2

Contents

Volume 5

Chapter 1

Sandy McLean glanced up from the book he was studying when there was a soft, tentative, tap on his bedroom door. He frowned at the interruption. 'Come in!'

It was his younger sister Laura who entered, her expression one of uncertainty. 'Am I disturbing you?'

Sandy sighed. Of course she bloody well was. 'That's all right,' he declared magnanimously. 'I was about to take a break anyway.' That was a lie. He waved in the direction of the bed. 'Take a pew.'

A glance at the clock on the mantelpiece told him it was just after nine-thirty p.m. He'd had his head down for over two hours now, and it

1

felt like it. The beginnings of a headache were starting to pulse inside his skull.

After she'd sat Laura gazed curiously around her. It had been a long time since she'd been in her brother's room, several years in fact. It was as messy as ever, she noted, tidyness certainly wasn't one of his finer points. In one corner an artist's easel had been set up, displaying a half-finished landscape in oils.

It suddenly struck Sandy how much his sister had grown of late. Why, she'd become quite the young lady, with a nice figure too, even if it was still in the budding stage. As he saw her nearly every day he wondered why he hadn't noticed that before. 'So, to what do I owe the honour?' he asked.

Laura shrugged. 'I don't know really. I just thought I'd come and talk to you, that's all. We so rarely get a chance.' When she saw his puzzled look, she added, 'Talk properly that is. Not just good morning, goodbye and that sort of thing.'

'I see,' he murmured, amused by this.

A silence followed during which she twined and intertwined her fingers in her lap.

'There must be something in particular?' he prompted.

'Not really. It's just ... well, although we're brother and sister we seem such strangers at times. I mean ... I mean ...' She trailed off, frowning. 'I've no idea what you actually get up to. Who your friends are. You know?'

For some reason that rather touched him. And she was right, they weren't exactly close. Not apart, but not close either. The usual brother and sister relationship, he supposed. 'I'm flattered,' he confessed.

Laura's face lit up, the tension between them suddenly broken. 'How are your studies coming along?'

How indeed, he thought bitterly, for he was in that sort of mood. How indeed! 'All right I suppose,' he replied non-committally.

'Just all right?'

Sandy bit back a waspish retort. Leaning sideways in his chair he pretended to yawn. 'Sometimes you can't see the wood for the trees.'

Laura slowly nodded. 'I understand. I find it the same with Latin. There are occasions in class when my head feels it's so crammed full nothing makes sense any more and that at any moment it might just explode.'

He regarded her with new interest, having forgotten she was even taking Latin at school. It dawned on him then how right she was about knowing so little about one another. 'Same with me,' he laughed.

Laura relaxed even further on hearing that, believing a bond, if only a tenuous one, had been established between them. 'Amo amas amat, amamus amatus amant,' she recited and giggled. 'Round and round like a dog chasing a cat.'

How old was she now? Sandy wondered, desperately trying to

work it out. Fifteen, yes that was it. Or was she fourteen? No, fifteen some months previously. 'Do you enjoy school? Overall that is?'

Laura considered that. 'Parts of it.'

'Like what?'

'English for example. The books we have to read. They can be fun.'

'And what else?'

'Art.'

A warm glow filled him. 'Are you any good?'

Laura shook her head. 'I'm rotten. No flair at all, at least that's what Mr McCormack my teacher says. And he's right. I can't draw or paint to save my life.'

Her eyes strayed over to the half-finished canvas on the easel. 'Unlike you. Now you have real talent. Everyone thinks so.'

Sandy couldn't resist it. 'Except Pa of course. And even if he did think I had something he'd never admit it in case it distracted me from what he wants me to do. Has decided I shall do.'

Laura could hear the bitterness in his voice. 'Is medicine so awfully bad?'

'Oh come on,' he chided softly. 'You've heard Pa often enough. He doesn't just want me to be a doctor but an eminent surgeon into the bargain. The goal he was never able to achieve himself.'

'You hate the idea, don't you?'

7

'Damn right I do,' he spat. 'But what choice have I? I can't go against Pa. That would be unthinkable. People like us don't go against their parents' wishes.'

'Poor Sandy,' she sympathised.

'The fact is, I totally loathe medicine. As for being a surgeon, eminent or otherwise, how ghastly having a job like that. A human butcher and plumber in other words.' He shuddered at the thought. 'No, whatever happens I'll be a family doctor the same as Pa, which is bad enough. Imagine having ill people around you every working day, especially horrible, smelly ones. Showing you their tongue, varicose veins, lumpy bits.'

'You're hardly being fair,' she countered. 'Medicine is about curing folk, making them better. Relieving pain and anxiety. I can't think of anything more rewarding than that.'

'Then you become a bloody doctor,' he snapped viciously. 'That might let me off the hook.'

Laura lowered her gaze, the cold fury of his eyes having frightened her. 'Sorry,' she mumbled. 'I was only trying to help.'

Sandy's anger subsided at the sight of her contriteness. 'I'm sorry too. I shouldn't have lost my temper like that.'

Laura reflected that Sandy had no idea he'd always been her idol, something of a God in her book. Her handsome big brother who, at least so it seemed to her, had always had something of an aura about him.

She'd always wished she was as pretty as he was handsome. But, sadly, that would never be. Though she was certainly not unattractive, and hopefully would improve as she got older, she'd never be as good looking as Sandy whom over the years she'd worshipped from afar.

'Can you keep a secret?' Sandy queried earnestly.

The abrupt change in conversation took her aback. 'Of course.'

'No, I mean it, really. Cross your heart and hope to die. All that sort of muck?'

Laura nodded, wondering what on earth he was about to confide to her.

Sandy got up from his desk and crossed over to where his painting things were, delving amongst the mess and clutter that was there. He grunted when he produced a nearly full half-bottle of whisky. 'If Ma or Pa knew I kept alcohol in the house they'd have a seizure,' he grinned.

Laura watched, a little in admiration she had to confess, as he poured himself a large one which he topped up from a bottle of lemonade standing on his desk.

'Bottoms up!' he toasted.

Sandy took a deep breath and then slowly exhaled. 'That's better. First of the day.'

He sat down again and smiled at her. 'Shocked?'

Was she? 'More surprised.' She gestured towards the bottle. 'That stuff is expensive. Where do you get the money from? I thought the allowance Pa gives you was only a small one.'

'It is,' Sandy confirmed. 'But I have ways and means. Other irons in the fire, so to speak.'

This side of him was a revelation to Laura. 'What sort of other irons?'

He winked conspiratorially. 'Ones that make me a fair old income on the side.' And with that he had another swallow. 'Can I try it?'

He stared at her in amazement. 'Don't be daft! Women don't drink whisky. At least, respectable ones don't.'

'Maybe not. But I'd still like to try it. I've only ever had sherry and that was nice.'

'Whisky is very different, Laura. Extremely intoxicating.'

'I appreciate that,' she replied patiently. 'I'm not asking for a glassful of the stuff, just a sip to find out how it tastes.'

Well, well, Sandy thought. There was more to his sister than he'd given her credit for. He'd always considered her something of a mouse. 'Are you absolutely certain?'

Laura's eyes were twinkling as she slid from the bed and made her way over to him. 'Absolutely. So what about it?'

With a shrug, he handed her the drink. 'Not too much mind. A sip, that's all.'

The fiery liquid, thankfully diluted by lemonade, almost made her choke.

13

'Not altogether unpleasant,' she pronounced eventually. 'In fact, I rather like it.' And with that she took a second, larger, sip.

'Here, hold on!' Sandy admonished, coming to his feet and taking the glass from her. 'I don't want you getting drunk.'

She giggled, already a little light-headed. 'It certainly beats sherry. By a mile.'

Sandy saw off what remained in the glass and promptly poured himself another. He suddenly realised he was enjoying her company.

'So, tell me about these irons in the fire you have,' Laura prompted.

In for a penny in for a pound, he thought. He'd already let her into his secret about keeping booze, why not

14

the rest of it? Staring into her face he reckoned she'd keep shtum. 'I run a book amongst the other students,' he informed her.

Laura frowned, not comprehending. 'What kind of book?'

'A racing book. I take bets on horses and dogs. It's extremely lucrative. Most of the time anyway.'

She was dumbfounded. 'Isn't that illegal?'

He shrugged. 'There's a need and I provide for it. Look at it that way. It doesn't harm anyone except the poor mugs who lose money and that's their fault for betting in the first place. Some of those chaps have pots of boodle coming from very well-off families. They can afford to lose.'

'But they don't lose all the time, surely?'

'Of course not. But overall they do. When it comes to betting there's only one person makes a profit at the end of the day, the bookie. Me, in other words.'

Laura, her mind whirling, returned to the bed. This was fascinating, exciting too. 'So how much do you make a week?'

Sandy pulled a face. 'Depends. It varies. And occasionally I'll be out of pocket. But on average, evening it out, I'd say roughly six quid a week, give or take a bob or two.'

Laura gasped. That was the weekly take-home pay of a working man. More actually. Considerably more in some cases. 'How long have you been doing this?'

'About a year now. Good idea, eh?'

She had to admit it was. 'As long as you know what you're doing.'

'Don't worry on that score. I do.'

She regarded him with now undisguised admiration. 'What do you spend it on?'

'This and that. And what I don't need I put in the bank. I've already put by a tidy sum, thank you very much. It just grows and grows.'

'Well done you,' she acknowledged. 'And what else?'

'How do you mean?'

'You said irons, plural.'

Sandy shook his head. 'Then it should have been singular. That's the one and only thing I have going on the side.'

'You're incredible, truly you are,' she stated wonderingly. 'And terribly clever.'

The compliment pleased him, enormously. He reflected on how liberating it was to have his own income and not have to rely totally on handouts from his father, who could be parsimonious to say the least. The very epitome of a tight-fisted Scotsman if ever there was.

'You won't breathe a word, will you?' he queried. 'You promised.'

'Not to a single soul,' she assured him.

'Good.'

Laura dropped her gaze, suddenly shy and hesitant again. 'I'm glad I came in to visit.'

'I'm glad you came in too. I was bored witless poring over these musty old books.'

'Can I come another time?'

Why not? he thought. Particularly if it gave him an excuse to stop studying for a while. 'If you like.'

'Then I will.'

Sandy glanced at the clock on the mantelpiece and decided he'd had enough 'work' for one night. He'd have another dram after Laura had gone and then take himself to bed.

As though reading his thoughts Laura pushed herself off the bed. 'I'd better go downstairs and say goodnight to Ma and Pa.'

'Just don't let them smell that whisky on your breath,' he warned. 'There'll be hell to pay if they do.'

'I hadn't thought of that,' she acknowledged. 'I'll make sure they don't.'

Laura headed for the door, then paused. 'Sandy?'

'What?'

Crossing quickly to him she kissed her brother on the cheek. 'Thanks.'

He didn't reply to that, merely smiled.

Moments later Laura had left, the door snicking quietly shut behind her.

Sweet, Sandy thought. He hadn't realised how sweet his sister could be. And how grown up she'd become. Well ... almost. For some reason he felt extremely happy, certainly better than he had before she'd appeared.

* * *

He couldn't sleep. He didn't know how long he'd been lying there, his mind churning. Instead of tiredness all he felt was a restless energy.

He idly toyed with the idea of getting up and painting. He hadn't touched his present canvas for five days now, thanks to all the damned studying he had to do for the forthcoming exams, which his father would be expecting him to do well in.

Sandy groaned in the darkness. There was about as much likelihood of that as there was of him sprouting wings. The trouble was he had no interest in Medicine, none whatsoever. And without interest how could he possibly learn and excel, the sense of application simply wasn't there. Duty, yes. But not application.

Christ, if only things were different, if only his father wasn't so insistent on his career, if only his father didn't expect so much of him, was more approachable—which he wasn't in the least—about a different profession.

If the choice had been up to him there wouldn't have been any contest. None at all. He'd have become a professional artist or at least had a damn good try at it.

All right, he knew what the odds were against success in that field, especially living in Glasgow where the arts weren't exactly given prominence. Token gestures were made, the art gallery for one, the theatres for another. Although in the case of the latter it was mainly shows of a variety and musical nature that were put on with the accent, literally, very heavy on the Scottishness of them. Harry Lauder would pack a theatre every time, he and other acts of the same, and similar, nature.

Ballet? That was a laugh. Not that he was very keen on it himself, but then how could he be as he'd never seen any. Despite this omission he was certain he would have hated it.

The most amazing thing as far as he was concerned was that Glasgow had a first-class art school housed in a beautiful building designed by Charles Rennie Mackintosh.

Given the choice that's where he would be, learning about and practising a subject he adored, instead of reading Medicine, being taught how to be a human butcher and plumber as he always described it, though never in the hearing of his father who would have been outraged and probably had apoplexy on the spot.

Of course, Father apart, the burning question to which he didn't have an answer, was if he was good enough ever to be a professional painter. There were times when he thought he might have enough talent, others when he considered it a ridiculous idea. An absurd presumption on his part.

One thing was certain, he'd have to work very hard at it, and learn a great deal, before he could ever possibly achieve such a lofty ambition.

A professional painter, living off the proceeds of his work! He sighed at the prospect. Following in the steps of Constable, Turner, Degas, Monet, Titian, and so many others. His skin felt prickly all over at the thought.

If only he could have gone to Art School then the question of his talent, or possible talent, might have been resolved one way or the other. But that wasn't to be; for the rest of his life it would merely remain a dream, the question of his potential forever a mystery.

No, his lot would be to be an amateur, painting for fun in his spare time, never as a livelihood.

Despair filled him; deep, black despair. That and anger that he couldn't have what he wanted above all else.

Sandy turned over onto his side to stare into the darkness, a darkness that seemed to reach deep inside him to the very depths of his being.

A Glasgow doctor with some pretty little mouse of a wife in time, and then no doubt children, all chaining him to the pillar of respectability that he so shied away from. He wasn't cut out for that, never in a million years. His soul was the rebellious sort, not destined to be confined by the restrictions of cosy hearth and home. His soul wanted to soar free, to wing its way wherever it wanted.

He groaned, knowing he was about as near sleep as he'd been earlier, in other words miles away. What torture it was lying there thinking about things, so desperately desiring something other than had been given him in life. He knew he should be thankful; his parents loved him, if in that peculiarly cold Calvinistic way; his father was well-to-do—money, within reason, was never a problem, there was always good food on the table and a roof over his head. Far removed from the life of many in Glasgow where there was so much grinding poverty and where the men, even when lucky enough to be in work, toiled in backbreaking graft in heavy industry such as the shipyards, steelworks, foundries and factories. Their only relief in life was to get roaring drunk on a Friday night, as they spent most of what they'd earned during the previous week, while at home the anxious wives fretted about how much of the pay packet would be left when their man finally came stumbling, usually incoherent, through the door.

And yet such men and women had a majesty about them, an incredible dignity etched indelibly on their faces. Pain, passion, sorrow, bewilderment, hope and anguish, anger and even, on occasion, the sheer joy of being alive. The indomitable human spirit showing through despite the crushing burden that was their day-to-day existence.

Like a bolt out of the blue it came to Sandy that that was what he should be painting, the working-class folk of Glasgow in all their grim reality.

'Oh!' he breathed aloud, excited at the thought. More than excited, exhilarated. He would sketch them, then come home and execute what he'd sketched in oils. Dull colours, greys and blacks and weak yellow, the colours that were Glasgow. No reds and blues here, or if so only sparingly, just the colours of dirt, grime, soot and flame.

He'd start sketching soon, he promised himself. That very weekend! Every available minute he could find.

And then his heart sank again, remembering the forthcoming exams he had to study for.

He swore long and vehemently.

* * *

'I'm worried about Alexander,' Harriet McLean declared to her husband Mathew across the breakfast table. Sandy and Laura had already excused themselves to go to university and school respectively.

Mathew, a tall thin man with a bony face and pencil-thin moustache, glanced at her in surprise. 'Why's that?'

Harriet considered her words carefully. 'He's so ... well, restless of late. Forever fidgety. And he doesn't look well, he's decidedly peaky.'

Mathew snorted. 'Speaking as a doctor, and his father, let me assure you there's nothing wrong with him. No doubt he's simply distracted about his exams. Perfectly natural,

30

my dear. Perfectly. And even if it isn't his exams, boys of that age are quite often odd, it's part of the growing-up process.'

'Do you really think so?'

'I'm certain of it. I seem to recall behaving somewhat similarly when I was twenty or thereabouts. It's just a stage, no more.'

Harriet remained unconvinced, though she didn't say so. Mathew hated being contradicted in any way. An iron tonic, she thought. Perhaps that might help. She had an appointment for a corset fitting later that morning. She made a mental note to drop into the pharmacist's directly afterwards.

* * *

It had been a good day for Sandy from the betting point of view. His net profit, after all bets had been settled, was seven pounds two and six for the week. Terrific.

He stopped outside The Clachan, a pub he often came to on a Saturday night as it was frequented by art students whom he enjoyed mingling with. Other medical students invariably went to the Union, the university bar where drinks were cheaper than elsewhere, but he much preferred The Clachan despite it being more expensive. He plunged into the heady atmosphere of cigarette smoke and loud conversation.

He went downstairs where the younger people gathered; upstairs was for the locals and older generation.

Right away he spotted Grant Bell, an acquaintance of his who lived out on the southside where he worked as an apprentice engineer. The pair of them had got talking in the pub one night, about philosophy of all things, and since then kept one another company when there.

'You all right? You're late,' Grant said, eyeing the large and ornate clock behind the bar.

'I'm fine. Got held up, that's all.' He'd been delayed waiting for one his punters he had to settle up with.

The barmaid, an ancient crone who must have been in her seventies, had dyed orange hair and a face like a prune. Her name was Myrtle. Sandy waved to catch her attention. 'A pint and a hauf,' he ordered when she bustled over. The hauf meant whisky.

Grant glanced about him. 'There's no decent talent in yet, but it's early. Something might turn up.'

Sandy grinned. Grant, not exactly the best-looking of men, was always trying to chat up the women who came down there and, to Sandy's knowledge, had never succeeded in getting off with one. 'Aye, you never know your luck.'

Grant's eyes flicked back to Sandy. 'Do I detect a hint of sarcasm in your voice, you cheeky sod?'

Sandy assumed an expression of innocence, knowing this was only good-natured banter. 'Not at all. As if I'd be sarcastic.'

Grant grunted, thoroughly enjoying himself. 'There's a table free. Do you fancy sitting down?'

It was unusual to get a table so late. 'You grab it and I'll be over in a mo'.' He drained the whisky as Grant moved away and instantly beckoned to Myrtle for a refill.

'This is Martin Benson, a pal of my brother's. They went to school together,' Grant said, introducing Sandy to a chap who appeared to have joined them.

Sandy placed his drinks on the table and extended a hand. 'Pleased to meet you, Martin. I'm Sandy McLean.'

'Aye, Grant just mentioned.'

Sandy took an instant liking to the man who had dark auburn hair and pale blue Celtic eyes. 'I see from

your scarf you're at the Art School,'
Sandy said as he sat down.

'That's right. Second year.'

'Enjoying yourself?'

Martin shrugged. 'I don't know about
enjoying, but it's good. Aye,
definitely that.'

Sandy was filled with envy and
jealousy which he did his best not to
show. How he wished he was there.

'And yourself?'

'Medical School.'

Martin nodded, but didn't make any
comment. 'Holy fuck, will you look at
what just walked in,' Grant swore
softly.

Sandy followed Grant's gaze to
fasten his own on the most stunning

of women who was with a chap slightly older than herself. Sandy guessed her to be in her mid-twenties. She was absolutely gorgeous. A real knockout.

'Lucky bastard, whoever he is,' Grant said, meaning the chap with the woman.

'You should see her stripped, she's really something then,' Martin declared in an offhand manner.

Both Sandy and Grant turned to stare incredulously at him. 'You've seen her naked?' Grant croaked.

'Quite a few times.' Martin grinned. 'The last being this afternoon.'

Sandy was dumbfounded, not knowing what to say to that. Martin was enjoying his little tease, all the more because it was true. 'She's

French, all the way from Gay Paree.
And her name's Sophie.'

French, Sandy mused. Now that he
thought about it she did have a
foreign look about her.

'How ... how ...?' Grant sort of
spluttered.

Martin laughed, deciding to put them
out of their agony. 'She models for
us in life classes.'

'Oh my God,' Grant whispered.

Sandy went back to staring at the
French woman, trying to envision
her nude. The picture he conjured up
made his throat constrict.

'If I get a chance I'll introduce you
later,' Martin declared. 'She's very
nice. You'll like her.'

'Like her? I'm already in love,' Grant sighed, causing the other two to laugh.

As it transpired that chance never came. Minutes later, Sophie and her male companion left.

Sandy's gaze followed her up every inch of the stairs until she disappeared from view.

Chapter 2

'Can I ask you something?' Laura turned to look at her friend, Madeleine Abercrombie. The pair of them were out for a Sunday stroll in Kelvingrove Park, something they often did when the weather was good. 'Of course, Madeleine.'

Madeleine cleared her throat, horribly aware that she was blushing. She and Laura had been best pals since their first-ever day at Laurel Bank School, and they were now as close as sisters. 'It isn't easy,' she mumbled. 'I mean, I'm embarrassed.'

Laura frowned. She indicated a nearby bench. 'Would you like to sit down?'

'Please.'

Once seated Madeleine fiddled with the fancy umbrella she was holding, which was similar to Laura's. As it was a beautiful day the umbrellas were for purely decorative purposes, part of a well-brought-up young lady's ensemble on such an occasion.

'So?' Laura prompted.

Madeleine glanced sideways at Laura, her cheeks now flaming scarlet. 'I wouldn't ask another single soul this. Honest.'

When her friend didn't go on Laura nodded, urging her to do so.

'I mean, I just couldn't,' Madeleine added in a tremulous voice. 'I'm flattered.'

Madeleine took a deep breath, and slowly exhaled. 'It's about men. I know absolutely nothing about them. What ...' she gulped. 'What goes on between them and women to make babies?' She turned away, breaking eye contact. 'I thought, well, you coming from a medical family, your father being a doctor and Sandy studying to be one, you were bound to know.'

'I see,' Laura replied quietly.

'I have tried to ... well I did broach it with Ma once, in a sort of roundabout way, but she wasn't forthcoming at all. In fact she couldn't have been more evasive.'

Laura could well believe that. Her own mother would have been just the same.

'Is it something to do with kissing and tummy buttons?' Madeleine queried.

Laura shook her head, her own knowledge on the subject extremely scant. 'No, it isn't. First of all, do you know the difference between men and women?'

'Sort of. Don't they have some kind of "thing" between their legs?'

'That's right. At least, so I understand.' Both girls pondered this mystery.

'How big is it and what does it look like?' Madeleine queried eventually.

'I don't exactly know,' Laura confessed. 'Although my father's a doctor he's about as much tight-lipped on those matters as your mother. My mother too come to that.

It's a sort of forbidden subject, as far as I'm concerned.'

Madeleine was momentarily distracted as a seagull flew overhead. At times there could be quite a few seagulls in the skies over Glasgow, it being built on a river and not far from the sea. She brought her attention back to Laura. 'What does he do with it, when making babies that is?'

Laura shook her head. 'I haven't the foggiest, but I'm certain it's nothing to do with your tummy button. And it can't be kissing, I've seen lots of people kiss.' She hesitated. 'Well, not many kiss in that way. Husband and wife so to speak. Kissing just wouldn't make any sense at all. Not if you think about it.'

'I suppose so,' Madeleine sighed.

'It's my belief, and I'm not sure where the idea came from, that a man's "thing" as you call it, is something like a spigot.'

Madeleine's eyes opened wide. 'A spigot?'

'Like you get on a barrel.'

Madeleine tried to imagine that between a man's legs, and couldn't. It was too ludicrous for words.

'A spigot,' Madeleine repeated, fighting back the urge to laugh.

This was a subject Laura had thought about herself from time to time, but how to find out details? 'Why are you asking anyway?' she queried.

Madeleine shrugged. 'Just curious, that's all.'

'What made you think about it now, today?'

Madeleine shrugged again and didn't reply.

They sat in silence for a little while, each lost in thought and conjecture. The silence was finally broken when Laura proposed they resume their walk.

'If I do find out I'll tell you,' Madeleine suddenly declared.

'And I you.'

'Promise?'

'Promise.'

Madeleine shivered slightly. 'I just hope it isn't too horrible, that's all.'

Laura hoped so too. Somehow she didn't think it could be. Or could it?

* * *

While Laura and Madeleine were taking their stroll, Sandy was down at the Broomielaw, right on the River Clyde, where the ships were loaded and unloaded. A hive of activity during the working week, now it was quiet with an air of serenity about it. Dotted around the quayside were tall, motionless cranes, like skeletal beasts having a well-earned rest.

Groups of men stood on the street corners chatting amongst themselves, passing the time of day. This was customary on a Sunday when there was absolutely nothing else to do. Glasgow entirely closed down for the Sabbath. Not a single pub, shop or any other convenience would be open; so strict was the rule that even the swings in the parks remained chained together.

Sandy was sitting on an empty wooden crate, sketch book in one hand, pencil in the other. The object of his attention was a circle of men opposite, each in a flat cap, collarless shirt, and standard black, or dark blue, 'Sunday best' suit. From the little he could overhear they appeared to be in a heated argument about the merits of various football clubs. One man in particular had caught Sandy's eye. He was old with a leathery, weather-beaten face, the lines on it etched so deeply they might have been chiselled. It was a face with incredible character.

Suddenly one of the men broke away from the circle and strode across the road, coming to a halt in front of Sandy to glare suspiciously at him.

'You. What the hell are you doin'?'

Alarm flared in Sandy, he hadn't expected this. 'Just drawing.'

'Drawin' what?'

Sandy prayed there wasn't going to be any trouble. The chap confronting him looked as if he could eat him for breakfast. He wasn't a big chap, but undoubtedly was as hard as nails, as most of these dockies were. 'Well, that man over there actually,' Sandy explained, pointing. 'The one smoking a pipe. Is that all right?'

'What do you want to draw him for?' The voice crackled with belligerence.

Sandy realised the group had fallen silent and were now, without exception, staring at him. 'He's got an interesting face. At least, I think so.' Sandy was doing his best to try to sound as friendly as possible.

The man was still glaring at him. 'Are you anythin' to dae with the Polis?'

That took Sandy aback. 'No, nothing,' he stuttered.

'Are ye sure?'

'Positive.'

'They come down here out of uniform sometimes trying to find things out. Snoopin' like, the bastards.'

'But why would they do that?'

The glare became an expression of foxy cunning. 'No ideas meself. Maybe they think there's the odd bit of jiggery pokery goes on from time to time. If they do they're barkin' up the wrong bloody tree.'

The man extended a rough and callused hand. 'See's that here.'

Sandy gave him the sketch book which the man looked at. After a few seconds he nodded his approval. 'That's Archie right enough. A good likeness.'

'Thank you,' Sandy acknowledged in relief.

The man flicked through the book, briefly studying the other sketches it contained. 'You have a talent, son, I have to admit.'

The eyes were suddenly back boring into Sandy's. 'And ye're nothin' to do with the Polis or Excise?'

'I'm a medical student,' Sandy explained. 'This is just my hobby.'

The man grunted. 'Wait here.' And with that he rejoined the others, the sketch book being given to the man Sandy had been drawing, and then to each man in turn.

The one who'd addressed him now returned and handed the book back to Sandy. 'Archie says his nose isn't as big as that, but otherwise thinks it's jim dandy.'

Sandy gave Archie a brief wave and was rewarded with a thumbs-up.

'If you want to draw faces and characters, then that pub down the road there, Betty's Bar,' the man said, pointing, 'is where you should be on a Friday and Saturday night.' The man laughed, a rasping rumble. 'Oh, you'll see some interesting faces in there awright. It's full of them.'

'Thank you. Maybe I will try it one weekend.'

'If you do and anyone attempts to gie you trouble just tell them you're a pal of Mick Gallagher. Got that?'

Sandy nodded. 'Got it. Thanks.'

'Same if you come here again on a Sunday. Any hassle then mention my name and you'll be awright.'

'Thanks again.'

Mick regarded him shrewdly. 'What's yours by the way?'

'Sandy McLean.'

'And where do you live, Sandy?'

'Lilybank Gardens in Hillhead.'

'Off the Byres Road?'

Sandy nodded. 'That's it.'

'Right then. Good luck to you, Sandy. Maybe see you in Betty's Bar.'

'Possibly.'

Sandy sketched for a while longer until the men broke up and went their various ways, Mick giving him a cheery wave as he walked off. Sandy returned the gesture.

Betty's Bar, Sandy mused as he headed for the nearest tram stop. It sounded a right dive. And fascinating.

* * *

It was later that week, during which Laura had often mulled over her conversation with Madeleine, that the idea popped into her head. Of course, she thought. Obvious really. The only question was, when would it be safe?

* * *

'What are you doing in here?'

Laura started, not having heard Sandy come in, engrossed as she was in one of his many art books. 'Sorry,' she mumbled.

Sandy closed the door behind him, angry at having found her in his bedroom without permission. 'I don't go into your room, so why come into mine?' he accused, eyes glinting his anger. Inviting her in when he was there was one thing, but this was quite another. It surprised him she'd taken the liberty. He waited for an explanation.

Laura closed the book and laid it on his desk. 'You're not usually home this early on a Sunday night.'

So this was planned, he realised, still mystified. 'The pub wasn't very good. Just one of those things. I got fed up and decided to leave.'

Laura was desperately trying to think of something other than the real reason for her being there.

Sandy crossed to his desk and stared at the book she'd been holding. 'Why the sudden interest in art?'

She shrugged.

Sandy went to where he kept his bottle of whisky hidden and proceeded to pour himself a large one. As far as he could remember it was at more or less the level he'd left it so it didn't appear that that was the motive behind her intrusion.

'I'm waiting,' he demanded harshly.

Laura felt completely wretched. It had taken her ages to get the opportunity to sneak off upstairs and now she'd been caught in the act. How on earth could she possibly tell Sandy why she was there? She would absolutely die of embarrassment if she did.

'Was it that book in particular?' Sandy probed.

She shook her head.

He was becoming exasperated. This just didn't make sense and was quite out of character for Laura. At least, as far as he knew it was.

Picking up the book he opened it and started to flick through some of the pages. For the life of him he couldn't work out what she'd been after.

'Can I go please?' she croaked.

'Not until you explain yourself.'

Tears appeared in her eyes. 'Please, Sandy?'

'If you're after something and I let you go then you'll just come back another time, so it's best dealt with here and now. Out with it, Laura.'

She couldn't look him in the face. This was awful. 'You'd laugh at me.'

'No I won't.'

'You would.'

He sighed, this was getting him exactly nowhere. But his curiosity had been aroused and he wasn't about to let her off the hook. 'Come on,' he cajoled. 'It can't be that bad. And I am your brother, don't forget. If there's something you want just say and you can have it.'

It was out of the question her taking any of his books to her own room, certainly not the ones she'd been searching for. There was too big a chance of discovery for her to do that.

Sandy decided to change tack. 'Would you like a sip of this whisky?'

Laura swallowed hard. 'If you don't mind.'

'Not in the least. But just a sip don't forget, apart from anything else you're under age.'

She had a sip and moments later felt better. Even that small amount of alcohol made her body relax and calmed her somewhat. On impulse, and despite what he'd said, she took a proper swallow.

'Hey!' Sandy exclaimed. 'I told you not to do that.'

She found herself smiling as he took the glass from her. She could get to like whisky and lemonade she thought. She could get to like it a lot.

'I can just go,' she stated. 'You can't keep me here.'

'No?'

'No.'

True, he reflected. He could hardly have a tussle with his own sister. Nor was there a lock on the door. 'Fine,' he replied. 'Leave. I'll simply have a word with Ma and you can explain to her what you were doing rummaging around in my room.'

'I wasn't rummaging,' she protested.

'I'd call it that. Going through my things is rummaging.'

'I wasn't going through your things,' she retorted fiercely. 'I was glancing through some of your books.'

'But why? That's the question.'

Would he tell Ma on her? She quite believed he would. 'Sod,' she whispered.

He wagged a finger at her. 'That's not a word a supposedly good little girl like you should use.'

'I'm not little,' she snapped back. 'I'm grown up.'

'At fifteen?' he mocked. 'Well almost,' she conceded. He was beginning to enjoy this.

Laura knew she'd been cornered. If she didn't tell Sandy why she was there then she'd have Ma to deal with, a far more daunting proposition. It was impossible to lie to Ma, she always saw right through you.

Laura took a deep breath, admitting defeat. How humiliating this was going to be. Totally and utterly. 'Let me have another sip,' she requested.

'No.'

'I need it to get the courage to speak.'

Sandy was now intrigued. He returned the glass to her and watched her have another swallow rather than the sip she'd asked for. Christ, he thought, half in admiration.

Laura went slowly to the fireplace and stood facing it, her back to Sandy. It would be easier this way.

'I'm still waiting,' he urged.

'Promise not to laugh?'

'I said I wouldn't.'

'You swear?'

'Oh for God's sake, Laura, I swear. Now get on with it.'

It was now or never, she thought, steeling herself. 'Madeleine and I were having a chat on Sunday, and we discovered ... discovered ...' She gulped. 'That we didn't know how babies were made. Or what a man's "thing" looks like.'

Sandy was stunned, this was not at all what he'd been expecting. Laura was right, his first impulse was to laugh, but, keeping to his word, he didn't.

'I see,' he murmured.

'It's so difficult to find out anything,' Laura went on. 'It's all such a mystery.'

Well, Sandy thought. Well, well, well. He finished off what remained in his glass then, returning to the bottle, poured himself a huge one to which he didn't add lemonade. He needed this one neat.

Laura remained silent, her back still to her brother.

Sandy was at a loss what to reply, wishing he hadn't persisted in making her confess. 'It is something of a taboo in polite circles,' he admitted. 'People just don't discuss it.'

'So how are we supposed to learn?' she queried.

Good question, he reflected. He'd heard of cases where women had gone to their wedding night blissfully unaware of what was about to happen. He was certain it must be different amongst the working classes where such matters would surely be more open, living as they so often did in overcrowded rooms with no privacy.

'I tried several of your medical books but didn't know what to look under,' Laura stated. 'Then I started leafing through your art ones trying to find a nude male. I couldn't. Females yes. But no males.'

A right pickle he'd landed himself in, he thought ruefully. What now? Explain what he could, or leave her in the dark?

'Sandy?'

Half the whisky in his glass vanished down his throat. He was becoming a little drunk, he realised. Good. Good. More whisky went the way of the other.

'Sit down,' he instructed. 'At the desk would be better,' he added when she moved towards his bed.

First things first, he thought, having decided to go through with this. It took him a few minutes to locate the book he was after, drawings by Michelangelo. Opening it at the appropriate place he laid it in front of Laura.

'That's a man's "thing", as you call it. The correct name for it is penis. It's referred to, especially amongst men, by many different pseudonyms, but penis is the correct, and medical, term.'

Laura was gazing at the drawing in fascination. How small it looked, she thought. Not at all frightening. 'So what does he do with it?'

Sandy cleared his throat. 'Have you, eh ... started having periods yet. Your monthlies?'

Her face flamed. 'Yes.'

'Well, you see ...'

When he'd finally finished Laura was staring at him in absolute horror. 'That's disgusting,' she whispered huskily. More whisky, Sandy told himself. He needed it. 'I mean, it can't be right.'

'I'm afraid it is.'

'And it ... gets a lot bigger?'

'When it fills with blood, engorged, which it does when the man gets excited.'

'And he actually ... inside?'

Sandy nodded.

'Surely it must hurt?'

'A bit the first time. But after that it's quite pleasurable. Certainly for the man, and often, I believe, for the woman. Though there are those who don't like it at all, the women that is, and only do it through a sense of duty. Or to simply procreate.'

Laura couldn't imagine ... She gave an involuntary shudder. 'Ma and Pa ...?'

'Had to have done otherwise you and I wouldn't be here.'

Laura was aghast. She didn't know what she'd expected to hear, but never this. She couldn't understand why such a barbarous act could possibly be pleasurable for either gender.

'So there you have it,' Sandy declared, glad that was over. Relieved in the extreme, to be exact.

'I still can't believe it,' Laura murmured.

'Well, it's true.'

'Laura! Where are you, dear?'

Laura instantly came to her feet. 'That's Ma calling. She must want me for something.'

She had one final look at the drawing in front of her. 'Thanks for explaining, Sandy. I appreciate it.'

'Glad to be of help.'

He watched her hurry from the room, allowing the door to close before his face split into a huge grin. Her expression, when he'd got down to the nitty gritty, had been absolutely priceless!

* * *

'If you don't get a move on you'll be late for surgery,' Harriet admonished Mathew who was engrossed in the morning newspaper.

He didn't bother glancing up. 'If I am late they can just wait. I want to finish this.'

Harriet gave an exasperated sigh. 'What's so important?'

'A house advertised for sale in Kelvinside. I'm reading the details.'

So that was it, Harriet thought. How many years was it now Mathew had coveted a house in Kelvinside, an area where the well-to-do lived?

Certainly many of the hospital specialists had houses there.

The trouble was, and why they'd never buy a house in Kelvinside, Mathew simply didn't earn enough money for them to do so. That didn't stop him desperately wanting one though.

'How much is it?'

'Doesn't say.'

'Whatever, it'll be outside our pocket.'

He lowered the newspaper a little to stare stonily at her over the top. 'There's no need to state the obvious.'

'Perhaps one day,' she smiled, trying to placate him. 'When our ship comes in.'

His reply was a grunt, both of them knowing that would never happen since there wasn't any ship to come in.

Mathew closed his eyes for a brief moment, living his dream. A dream that would never, could never, be.

'I do believe I'll have another cup of tea,' he declared, opening his eyes again. Now he certainly would be late. Truth was, he didn't give a damn. Let the hoi polloi wait, he'd see them when he was good and ready, not before.

* * *

Professor Leishmann might be a brilliant surgeon, but his lecture delivery was the most boring imaginable. He intoned, dropping the ends of his sentences in the way that many ministers often do. Sandy, listening to him, was having the utmost difficulty in not dropping off to sleep.

Leishmann droned on. 'Mechanically, the thorax resembles a syringe; the diaphragm acts as the piston, or plunger, being pulled down by its own contracting muscle and recoiling upwards as it relaxes. By an alteration of the ribs ...'

Sandy had long since stopped taking notes, idly doodling instead. Suddenly the memory of the French woman in The Clachan that night flashed into his mind and before he knew what he was doing he was attempting to draw her likeness.

What a cracker, he recalled as his pencil flew. He paused every so often to scrutinise his effort.

That jammy bastard, Martin Benson, he thought, having her as a nude model in life classes. He'd have given anything just to attend a single one.

When he had her face to his satisfaction, the eyes particularly good, he thought, he began drawing what he imagined she might be like with her clothes off. All sheer speculation of course, but fun.

The rest of the lecture just whizzed by.

* * *

'I found out,' Laura announced to Madeleine, as the pair of them walked home from school. 'Found out what?'

'How babies are made and what a man's "thing" looks like.'

Madeleine stopped walking to stare at Laura. 'How?'

'My brother told me and even showed me a picture of a man's thing, the correct name for which is penis, by the way, in one of his art books.'

'He did!'

Laura nodded.

'What's the penis like?'

A spigot, as I said. At least that's the best way I can describe it.

'And what does he do with it to make babies?' Madeleine demanded eagerly.

Laura took a deep breath. 'I still find it hard to believe this is true myself, but Sandy swears it is.'

Madeleine listened open-mouthed as Laura recounted what Sandy had told her.

Chapter 3

Now that he was actually here Sandy wasn't at all sure it had been a good idea. The Broomielaw at night was a darkly menacing place, with the threat of danger lurking all around.

Come on, don't be such a big jessie, Sandy told himself. If it's too awful you can just turn round again and leave. He pushed open the badly chipped door and went inside.

The smell that hit him was a combination of spilt beer and rank human sweat. Was it his imagination or had every eye in the place suddenly focused on him?

There were three barmen, all tough-looking characters. The one he approached had what he surmised to be a razor scar running the full length of his cheek down to his mouth. The flesh around it was puckered and drawn.

The barman appeared mildly surprised to see him. 'Aye, what do you want?' the barman demanded.

'A pint and a hauf please.'

'Which beer?'

Sandy, heart thumping, glanced at what was on offer and selected one.

'Never seen you in here before?' the barman queried as he poured the pint.

'First visit. It was recommended to me by Mick Gallagher.'

The barman's expression changed to something approaching friendly. 'Are you the artist chap?'

Sandy liked that, being called an artist. 'Yes, I am.'

'Mick warned us you might be coming in. Said we were to look out for you.' He lowered his voice fractionally. 'It can be a wee bit rough in here at times, if you get ma meanin'.'

Sandy got it all right. 'Thanks for the tip.'

The barman looked him up and down. 'You do stand out in those posh clothes.'

Sandy hardly considered them posh. But there again, they weren't a workman's clothes. 'They're all I've got,' he apologised.

'Mick'll be in later. He'll no doubt want to say hello.'

'Do you know him well?' Sandy inquired as the barman placed his pint in front of him.

The barman grinned, a grotesque leer on account of the scar. 'I should do since I'm married to his sister Kathleen. Me and Mick are great pals.'

'So you're his brother-in-law.'

'That's it.'

Sandy paid and the barman moved off to serve another new arrival. Glancing round Sandy spotted an empty table in a corner and decided to sit, thinking to make himself as inconspicuous as possible.

He was amazed at the number of single women present, which was very unusual for a Glasgow pub. Normally they would only come in with their husband or boyfriend, or in groups, two at the least. Single women were rare. And then he had a thought. Unless ...? That could be a possibility, he decided.

As it got towards eight o'clock the pub began to fill rapidly, the men clearly intent on enjoying themselves after a hard week's graft.

Mick had been right, there were some extremely interesting faces and characters here. A tall blond man was speaking to an equally blond male companion in what sounded to Sandy like Swedish, or possibly Russian. The man would have made a splendid Viking, Sandy decided.

A couple of brown men burst in through the door, Laskars off one of the ships Sandy presumed. They seemed good natured enough.

A fat woman caught Sandy's attention. Her face was raddled with old smallpox scars while one of her eyes had a cast to it. Her bosom was absolutely enormous and she was drinking pints. Another first for Sandy who'd never seen a woman drink pints before.

'It's yersell, Bella,' another woman called out, swaying drunkenly over to the fat woman and plonking herself down beside her. They immediately fell into an animated conversation peppered with swear words.

Mick and a couple of his cronies came in and went straight to the bar where his brother-in-law immediately muttered something to him. Mick glanced over, spotted Sandy and waved. Sandy acknowledged him.

A few minutes later Mick came across carrying two full pints. 'You made it, I see,' he smiled.

'I did that.'

'What do you think?'

'It certainly lives up to what you said.'

Mick laughed and pushed a pint to Sandy. 'That's for you.'

'Thank you. You're very kind.'

'And you're helluva polite,' Mick laughed again. 'We're no used to that in here.'

Sandy didn't know what to reply to that, so said nothing.

'There's someone I want you to meet,' Mick went on. 'He'll be out in a minute or two. Tommy's gone to tell him you're here.'

Sandy was mystified; who would want to meet him, and why? 'Is Tommy your brother-in-law?' Mick nodded.

'He says you and he are great pals.'

'We are that. Used to work alongside each other, but then he got this job which he prefers because of his rheumatism. Indoors see.'

Sandy wanted to ask how Tommy had got his scar, but decided that might not be wise. It could be construed as offensive. He was about to ask, instead, who wanted to meet him when a middle-aged and reasonably well-dressed, in the sense that he wore a collar and tie, man emerged from behind the bar heading in their direction.

Mick came to his feet. 'Aye, there you are, Bob. This is that Sandy McLean I mentioned.' To Sandy he explained, 'Bob owns the pub.'

Sandy also came to his feet. 'Pleased to meet you, Bob.'

'And me you, son. Sit down, sit down, no need to stand on ceremony.' He caught one of the barmen's eye and held up three fingers.

'I hope you don't mind me joining you,' Bob smiled, sitting alongside Sandy. 'Not in the least.'

'It's just that Mick says you're a bit of an artist, like?'

There it was again, being called an artist. He loved it. 'I'm really a medical student, art is merely something of a hobby.'

Bob regarded him shrewdly. 'Mick tells me you did a right good likeness of Archie. I don't suppose you have it with you?'

'As a matter of fact I have.' He'd brought along his sketch book in the hope he might be able to use it while there.

'Can I see it, son?'

'Of course.' Again Sandy was mystified. He leafed through the book till he found the page with Archie on it, then handed the book to Bob.

Bob studied it for a few moments. 'Aye, right enough. It is good. Archie to the life.'

'I told you!' Mick stated triumphantly.

Bob focused again on Sandy. 'I have a wee proposition for you, son.'

'Proposition?'

'Mick's idea. I've spoken to some of the lads, regulars like, and they all agree.'

The conversation was interrupted by a barman who laid three drams on the table, one of which Bob placed beside Sandy's pint, another alongside Mick's. 'On the house.'

Mick lifted his glass. 'Slainthe!'

Sandy and Bob followed suit.

'My own bottle, best malt,' Bob explained to Sandy, and chuckled.

'It's certainly good stuff,' Sandy acknowledged.

Bob became businesslike again. 'Archie has been coming in here man and boy, long before I ever bought the place, and the owner before me. Well, the thing is he's due to retire next month and we wanted to do something a bit special for him. Something more than just getting him pissed for the night. That's where Mick comes in, he suggested we get you to do a proper portrait of Archie which we'll have framed and hang on the wall. He'll be dead chuffed with that, so he will.'

'A portrait,' Sandy mused, taken aback.

'No' an oil thing, but pencil like you've already done. Though this time proper like and a decent size. What do you say?'

'Will you do it, Sandy?' Mick urged.

Sandy didn't see why he couldn't. 'Next month?'

Bob nodded. 'Three weeks the night to be exact.'

That wouldn't give him long, Sandy thought. Not if the drawing was to be framed as well. 'Will Archie be in later?' he queried.

'Should be,' Bob replied. 'Usually is on Fridays.'

'I need to get closer to him, get a better look at his face. What I did before was from a distance. To do it properly I'd need more detail.'

'So you'll do it?' Mick smiled.

'Honestly, it would be my pleasure.'

'That's settled then. Except for the money,' Bob declared.

Money? He hadn't expected that.

'What will you charge?' Bob asked.

Sandy hadn't the faintest notion, never having been paid for a drawing or painting before. His brow furrowed as he thought about it. 'Tell you what,' he said at last. 'Let's wait and see what you think of what I produce. If you don't like it, fine. If you do, then you can decide what it's worth. How's that?'

'Fair enough. It's a deal,' Bob declared, extending a hand which Sandy shook.

'Talk of the devil,' Mick said quietly, and nodded towards the door where Archie had just appeared.

Mick came to his feet. 'Leave this to me, Sandy. I'll get him close enough for you, and keep him there for a while. Awright?'

For the rest of the night pints kept turning up on Sandy's table, compliments of the management.

* * *

Sandy was smiling broadly as the tram taking him home rattled along its rails. A commission! Well, that's what it was. Of course it was. A real commission, his first ever.

What a night it had been, he couldn't remember the last time he'd enjoyed himself so much. And most of it for free too, a bonus if ever there was.

True to his word Mick had manoeuvred Archie close to where Sandy had been sitting giving him plenty of opportunity to study the older man's face. Without it being noticeable he'd even managed to make a few rough line sketches to go from when he came to do the job properly. And Archie had been right in his original criticism, his nose wasn't as big as Sandy had initially thought, as viewed from across the street!

A commission! He couldn't wait to get started. All going well he'd deliver it the following Friday night which would leave Bob enough time to get it framed.

Providing Bob liked it that is, which Sandy fervently hoped he would.

* * *

93

Mathew sighed in annoyance as he laid aside the latest edition of the medical journal The Lancet he'd been reading.

'Are you aware you've been staring at me, on and off, for what must have been the past hour?' he accused Laura.

Laura blushed. 'Sorry, Pa.'

Harriet, who'd also been reading, glanced up at them both in surprise. 'Were you staring, Laura?'

'I wasn't aware of it, Ma,' she lied.

'Well, you were,' Mathew snapped. 'Most disconcerting. I was beginning to think I must have sprouted horns for you to find me so fascinating.'

'I suppose I was just daydreaming,' Laura lied further, mortified at having been caught out. The truth was she'd been trying to imagine her father and mother doing what Sandy had described you had to for making babies, and totally failing.

It was simply so absurd, obscene almost. Pa putting his penis inside Ma didn't bear thinking about, and yet that's exactly what must have happened.

Sandy had said some women found it pleasurable, did Ma? And what about Pa, did he?

Surely that sort of thing was long in the past now she and Sandy were here. How old were her parents, after all? Pa was somewhere in his late forties, Ma a few years younger. Yes, they had to be well past that kind of business.

Unless they wanted another child, but, at their age, it was most unlikely they did. At least to her way of thinking. Quite ridiculous.

Her thoughts were interrupted by the sound of the telephone ringing outside in the hallway. During the day Morag, their maid, would have answered it, but she'd gone home some hours previously, as had Cook, as neither of them lived in.

'Probably for me,' Mathew grunted, heaving himself out of his chair where he'd been most comfortable. He left the room, still somewhat irritated by Laura having been staring at him for so long. A strange child, he thought. Always had been. And certainly far too wilful for her own good. He had no idea where that had come from. Not him, nor Harriet either. Harriet could be strong minded, stubborn even, but never wilful.

'Oh dear, I hope he hasn't got to go out,' Harriet said to Laura. 'But there we are, it's a doctor's lot I suppose if he has. People don't realise how disruptive these things can be to home life. They just haven't any idea.'

Laura smiled in sympathy, wondering why her mother still made a fuss over something that had been happening regularly for as long as she could remember.

Mathew returned a few minutes later. 'Mrs McEvoy's baby is arriving and the midwife wants me there as she thinks there are going to be complications.'

'I don't suppose you know how long you're likely to be?'

Mathew shook his head. 'These matters are a law unto themselves.'

'You'll miss supper then?' That was a snack the Scots have usually around nine-thirty to ten shortly before going to bed. It invariably consists of sandwiches and savouries accompanied by tea or coffee.

'I should imagine.'

Harriet shook her head sadly. 'Pity. Cook has left out a particularly nice one too.'

'I may have a bite when I get back, so don't throw out what's left.'

Mathew went to Harriet and pecked her on the cheek. 'Toodle-oo then.'

'Toodle-oo, darling.'

For the rest of that evening Laura made a point of hardly looking at her mother, then only when spoken to, and certainly not staring.

* * *

It was finished, Sandy thought triumphantly. And he was pleased with it, even if he said so himself. He decided to put it up on his easel, covering the painting of the landscape which he still hadn't completed. Now that he came to think about it, he doubted he would. He'd lost all interest in the subject.

He frowned when there was a tap on the door. 'Who is it?'

'Laura. Are you studying?'

He was about to reply that he was, then changed his mind. 'Come in!'

'I hope I'm not disturbing,' she apologised as she came in the room.

'No, you're not.'

She caught sight of the drawing, and smiled. 'I say, that is good,' she declared, pointing. 'Do you think so?'

She went closer and peered at it. 'Yes, I do. Who is he?'

'My first commission,' Sandy couldn't help boasting.

Her eyes opened wide. 'Commission! You mean someone is actually going to pay you for it?'

'Well, don't sound so surprised,' he replied, a trifle miffed.

'Sorry. But as you just said it is your first ever. Don't be so touchy.'

He ignored that. 'His name's Archie and he's a dock worker. I've been commissioned by the landlord of his local pub. It's a retirement present from the landlord and the regulars.'

'How much are they paying you?' she queried, both fascinated and curious.

'That hasn't been decided yet,' he admitted. 'It depends on whether or not they like it, and if so, how much they think it's worth.'

'About a hundred pounds, I'd say.' Sandy burst out laughing. 'I wish!'

'Well, it's as good as any professional artist could do. I've seen the paintings in the art gallery and they're certainly no better.'

'You're talking nonsense, Laura,' he protested. 'No I'm not. I mean every word.'

If only it was true, he thought. It would be a dream come true.

Laura rightly interpreted the look on his face. 'Would you really like to be a professional artist instead of a doctor?' she queried quietly.

Sandy took a deep breath. 'More than anything. Medicine bores the pants off me. Always has done. I wouldn't be at medical school if it wasn't for Pa.' He shrugged. 'But I've already told you all that.'

'Poor Sandy,' she sympathised. 'I knew you enjoyed your drawing and painting but never guessed you felt that way about it.'

His expression became melancholy, the elation of her compliment seeping out of him. 'It's just not to be, that's all. All there is about it. Sadly.'

She went to him and touched him ever so lightly on the arm. 'I am sorry.'

'Not as sorry as me. I suppose it's simply that some things in life just aren't to be.'

Laura looked at the drawing again, marvelling at how lifelike the portrait was. She half expected the man to open his mouth and speak to her. 'Maybe you'll draw me sometime,' she heard herself say.

'Maybe,' he prevaricated.

The tone in his voice told her he was reluctant. 'I shouldn't have asked.

Very presumptuous of me,' she apologised.

'No no, that's all right.' He could see he'd hurt her feelings, after her being so kind to him too. He decided to explain.

'Perhaps in a few years, Laura, when your face has acquired a few lines. At the moment it's bland because you're so young. Can you understand that?'

'You're saying it's not interesting enough?'

'Let me put it this way, I think it will be far more so when you're older,' he replied tactfully.

She accepted that, realising he was trying to be gracious. 'Well, I still think that old man is wonderful and I can't see how these people can fail to like it. And, in my opinion, no matter what they pay you they'll be getting a bargain. So there.'

He grinned, touched by her words and sentiments. 'I think this calls for a drink,' he announced.

'From your secret cache?'

'Exactly,' knowing that her comment was meant to tease. Laura watched him as he hunted out his bottle and poured himself one, adding the usual lemonade. 'Cheers!' he toasted. 'Can I have a sip?'

He wagged a finger at her. 'You're getting a taste for this stuff,' he admonished.

She knew that to be so. 'A sip won't harm,' she argued.

'Last time you were here you were having swallows instead of sips,' he reminded her.

Her reply to that was a broad smile.

'Anyway,' he went on. 'Why are you here? It wasn't about my drawing.'

'Can I sit down?'

'If you wish.'

'After a sip?'

How could he refuse when she'd been so nice about his drawing. 'Just one then. And I'm holding onto the glass so make sure that's all you have.'

When she'd had that she took herself over to his bed.

'Well?' he prompted.

'It's to do with our last chat.'

He inwardly groaned. Not that again!

'I'd like some more information.'

'Go on,' he said slowly.

'It's detail really.'

'I'm listening.'

'You said a man's penis gets bigger when he's about to ...' She trailed off.

'Yes.'

'How big?'

Christ, he thought. What a question. He couldn't believe he was actually having this conversation with his young sister. Or any woman, come to that.

'I suppose it depends,' he said evasively.

Laura looked puzzled. 'Why?'

'They vary in length. Some can be longer than others. Or so I'm led to understand.'

'You don't really know?' She frowned.

'Bloody hell!' he muttered in exasperation. 'No, I don't. Men don't exactly go around comparing their willies with one another.' He glared at her. 'Willies, that's one of the many pseudonyms I mentioned.'

Willies, willy? A far nicer word than penis. Less threatening somehow. And certainly less clinical. 'Don't get cross with me, Sandy. I'm only trying to find out about these things. Surely there's nothing wrong with that?'

He couldn't disagree, but it was so embarrassing.

'So what would an average be?'

He returned to the whisky bottle and topped up his glass, praying this was the last time she'd come to his room asking questions like these. 'Average?'

'Show me.'

That alarmed him. 'How do you mean, show you?'

'With your hands, silly. Hold them apart at the appropriate length.'

Relief rushed through him. For a horrible moment there he'd thought she was asking him to expose himself. Heaven forbid! He was only too well aware how intently Laura was studying him. 'Is this necessary?'

'Please, Sandy? I'm curious,' she pleaded, voice loaded with cajoling femininity.

There seemed to be nothing else for it. Laying down his glass he held his inwardly turned palms roughly the right distance apart.

Laura had paled. 'That can't be right.'

'Well it is. Satisfied now?'

She gulped. 'And that's what ...'

'Yes,' he interjected.

It was impossible, she thought. Something that large could never ... Her mind was reeling.

Sandy suddenly smiled, struck by the ridiculousness of this. Picking up his glass again he had another swallow. The whole thing was somehow surreal. 'Don't forget that where a willy goes in is where the baby comes out. It expands. All quite natural, I assure you.'

When he saw the expression on Laura's face he went to her. 'Here, have another sip.'

'Thank you,' she whispered when she'd had it. 'Anything else? If so, let's get it over and done with.' Laura shook her head. 'Are you sure?'

Laura slid off the bed. 'I'd better go.'

'Thanks for being so complimentary about my drawing.'

She nodded, but didn't reply.

'Bloody questions,' he muttered when she was gone. Talk about being put on the spot!

He glanced over at his desk and the books piled there. The exams were only a few weeks away, he really should get down to a bit of study, but as always was reluctant to do so.

But he had to, he reminded himself. Simply had to. But that didn't make it any the easier.

* * *

Nervous as anything, Sandy halted outside Betty's Bar. He'd come to deliver the drawing which he was carrying rolled up inside a cardboard cylinder. 'Oh well,' he thought, 'best get on with it.'

He was greeted by a smiling Tommy when he went up to the bar, the scar making Tommy's grin as grotesque as ever.

'Is Bob around?'

'Aye, he's out the back.'

'Could you tell him I'd like a word?'

'Of course.'

Tommy returned a few moments later with Bob in tow. 'Hello, son.' Bob nodded.

Sandy held up the cylinder. 'I've brought it.'

The pub was near deserted as it had only been open a short time. 'Let's have a dekko then,' Bob replied.

Sandy shook the drawing free and unrolled it.

'Excellent,' Bob pronounced after what, to Sandy, seemed an eternity. 'You've done a grand job there. Done Archie proud.'

Sandy almost sagged where he stood. His first commission and it had been approved! Elation sang within him.

Bob clapped him on the shoulder. 'Couldn't be more pleased. This will look terrific when it's framed and up on the wall. Now what do you want, on the house?'

When Sandy left the pub a little later he felt as if he was walking on air.

Chapter 4

Sandy was ambushed the moment he got home by Laura, who had been keeping an eye out for him and listening for the door. 'Well?' she demanded. 'Did he like it?' Sandy, still euphoric, nodded.

Laura squealed with delight. 'That's wonderful! I told you he would.'

On impulse he gathered her into his arms and swung her round. When her feet touched the floor again he kissed her on the cheek. 'Thanks for saying what you did the other night, about it being good.'

'But it was true!' she replied, eyes shining.

'I can't wait to see it framed.'

'I wish I could too.'

Sandy laughed. 'That'll never be, I'm afraid. Betty's Bar isn't exactly the kind of place for you. Far too rough.' He lowered his voice. 'You should see one of the barmen, a razor scar from here to here.' He indicated the length of the mark on his own face.

'Really!'

'All sorts goes on in there, though I haven't seen that side of it yet. They're all hard as nails.'

Laura's expression became one of concern. 'You will be careful, I hope?'

'Don't worry, I'm protected. Firstly by my new acquaintance Mick Gallagher, secondly by the landlord and his barmen. If anyone tried anything on they'd soon be out on their ear.'

'How exciting,' Laura enthused. 'I'm quite jealous.'

It was exciting, Sandy reflected. 'The people are all so ...' He groped for words. 'Different to what I'm used to. These are real people, workers who graft with their hands for a living.'

'Do women go there?'

'Oh yes, and you should see them. Scary to say the least. And I do believe some are ...' He suddenly hesitated, was this what he should be confiding in his sister, and would she even know what he was talking about?

'Go on,' she urged.

'Prostitutes.'

Laura had vaguely heard the expression, but wasn't at all knowledgeable about what a prostitute did. 'I see,' she replied gravely, pretending she did know. Or at least had an inkling.

'At least that's my guess.'

Something else she was going to have to find out about, Laura thought. She'd look the word up in the dictionary.

'What are you two up to?' Harriet demanded, appearing in the hallway.

'Nothing, just talking,' Sandy answered.

Harriet's eyes narrowed. 'It looks to me as if you're up to something.'

Sandy laughed. 'What on earth would we be up to? That's nonsense.'

It was still a bit peculiar, Harriet thought. Normally that pair didn't have much time for one another, far less being deep in conversation as they appeared to have been.

'Well, you'd better get ready for dinner. It'll be served shortly,' Harriet stated as she swept away.

'I am delighted for you,' Laura smiled to Sandy. 'Let's just hope this was the first of many commissions.'

Sandy matched her smile. 'I doubt it. But it's a lovely idea.'

'See you at dinner,' Laura said and headed after her mother. Later she intended getting out her dictionary.

* * *

'I'd like you to meet the wife,' Mick Gallagher declared. 'Beryl, this is Sandy who I've told you about. And Sandy, this is Beryl.'

Sandy had already risen from his chair and now shook hands with Beryl Gallagher. Considerably younger than Mick, Sandy noted. And pretty, in a rather obvious way. He couldn't help notice, well it was rather on display, how well built she was in the bust department.

'Pleased to meet you,' Sandy said.

'And me you. I'm dying to see this picture of yours. Mick says it's terrific.'

'You sit with Sandy for a minute while I get them in,' Mick nodded to her. He eyed Sandy's nearly empty pint. 'Another?'

'Please.'

'And a dram to go with it?' Sandy's expression was affirmative. 'Right, won't be a tick.'

Sandy found Beryl's cheap scent almost overpowering. Despite the vulgarity of it he thought it was very sexy. As was Beryl herself. Beryl pulled out a packet of cigarettes and offered Sandy one. 'No thanks, I don't.'

'Nasty habit, but I love my fags. I go mental when I haven't got any. Wednesdays and Thursdays usually, just before pay day. First thing I do when I get his money is shoot off down to the shop for some Woodies.' She laughed, a surprisingly deep sound. 'Pathetic, isn't it?'

Sandy decided to be diplomatic. 'I can't say really as I don't smoke, and never have. But I do know it can be quite addictive.'

'Aye, too bloody true,' she laughed, her green eyes sparkling.

Like Mick, she was of Irish descent, Sandy realised. She had an Irish look about her. And Catholic too no doubt, the minority in Glasgow, and hated by many Protestants.

Beryl leant a fraction closer. 'Mick tells me you're going to be a doctor. Is that right?'

'Hopefully.'

'That's fabulous,' Beryl enthused. 'I wanted to be a nurse mesell, applied to a few hospitals too when I was younger. But they didnae want to know. Turned me down flat. I don't think I was posh enough for them.'

She was probably right, Sandy reflected. Hospitals were notoriously snooty about who they took to train as nurses. Beryl's broad Glasgow accent would have ruled her out straight away.

He was saved replying to that by Mick returning with their drinks. 'I'll join you both in a minute,' Mick said. 'I just want to speak to someone first.'

Sandy watched Mick move away, edging his way through the crowd that was rapidly beginning to gather. 'Good man, your husband. I like him,' Sandy declared.

Beryl picked up her gin. 'Oh, he's a good man right enough. One of the best. Mind you, he hasn't been the same since his accident.'

Sandy frowned at her. 'What sort of accident?'

'At work. It happened a couple of years ago. He got crushed when an eejit operating a crane dropped a wooden crate on him. He was laid up for three months and more. Hard times those.'

'He seems all right now though.'

'Still got a wee bit of a limp, especially when he's tired. And both his legs are scarred.'

Sandy's expression was one of sympathy. 'At least you can both be thankful it wasn't worse.' He said that knowing men were killed on the docks, an ever-present occupational hazard.

'Aye, there is that,' Beryl replied slowly. 'The worst part was it wasn't only his legs that got crushed, if you get ma meanin'. As I said, he's never been the same since.'

Sandy realised the implication of that and was absolutely appalled she'd confided such intimate information to him on such short acquaintance.

'It makes life difficult,' Beryl added quietly, staring into her gin.

Sandy could well imagine. He had absolutely no idea how to reply to what he'd just been told.

In a catlike way Beryl glanced sideways at him. 'Tragic, huh?'

Sandy nodded, not meeting her gaze.

'It gets me down at times. I'm so young too. Only twenty-five. Just twenty-five in fact, last month.'

Sandy would have thought her older by several years at least. But then the working class often looked older than their actual age due to the conditions they lived under, which were often harsh to say the least. He enjoyed a life of ease and luxury by comparison.

'Do you have a ladyfriend yersell, Sandy?' she asked, apparently innocently.

Christ, he wished Mick would get back. He shook his head.

'That surprises me. A good-lookin' chap like you. I'd have thought the lassies would have been fallin' over themselves. Apart from anything else a budding doctor is quite a catch.'

'I don't have any time for girls. I seem to be either at medical school or home working,' he lied. Of course he had time to spare, otherwise he wouldn't have been there.

Beryl leant even nearer, affording him a view down her cleavage. 'That's a cryin' shame, so it is. Some poor lassie is missing out. And you such a big strappin' lad too.'

Strapping lad! He'd hardly have described himself as that. Her scent was so strong this close it was beginning to make his head swim.

'I hardly think so,' he muttered in a strange, strangulated voice. Mick! he silently screamed. Get back here!

Beryl reached across and laid a hand over his. 'Well, I do.'

A pint was suddenly plonked down on the table. Mick had rejoined them. Thank God for that, Sandy thought in relief. She'd have been propositioning him next.

'Sandy's just been tellin' me he disnae have a ladyfriend,' Beryl said smoothly, switching her attention to Mick. 'Maybe we can do something about that.'

'Don't be daft, woman. There's nobody round here would interest the likes of him. He's a cut above this lot. Educated properly and that. Well spoken. So get a grip.'

There was amusement reflected in Beryl's eyes as she lit another cigarette. 'Aye, you're probably right.'

'Of course I am. Stands to reason. That so, Sandy?'

How did he answer that without causing offence? He didn't reply, merely shrugged and had a long pull from his pint.

'Archie!' the call suddenly went up. 'The old bugger's here at last!'

Sandy could just make out Archie through the crowd, people clapping him on the back and shaking his hand as he made for the bar. From what he could see Archie looked both moved and surprised.

Bob appeared from the rear of the pub carrying the framed drawing wrapped in brown paper. A few moments later he cried out in a foghorn voice for silence.

The speech was relatively short, reminding everyone that Archie had been coming into Betty's man and boy and was a model customer to boot. A glare intimating that many of them weren't got a loud laugh.

Eventually Archie was presented with the drawing which he unwrapped with hands that trembled with emotion. After staring at the drawing in astonishment for almost a full minute he held it up for all to see, earning a huge round of applause.

'And it's to go on the wall above Archie's favourite seat!' Bob informed everyone, which received another huge burst of applause.

Bob placed the drawing behind the bar where it could be viewed by all and sundry as the night wore on. Tommy meanwhile slipped out from behind the bar holding an empty pint pot.

'I think we can safely say your drawing is a success.' Mick beamed at Sandy.

'Aye, look at Archie, he's right chuffed,' Beryl added. 'Mick's idea in the first place,' he informed her. 'Aye, he mentioned.'

Tommy was going from customer to customer, having a quiet word with each. As Sandy watched he saw money tinkling into the pot, in one case a ten-bob note.

'I'm goin' for a gander at the drawing,' Beryl announced. 'I could use another gin in the meantime.'

'That's my shout,' Sandy said quickly, also rising. It was with relief that he went one way, Beryl the other.

When Sandy returned it was to find Archie waiting for him, the old man misty eyed.

'I believe I've got you to thank for yon drawing, son,' Archie stated gruffly.

'I did it, yes.'

'It's one helluva retiral momento. Although it's stayin' in the pub I'll treasure it to my dyin' day. I just wanted you to know that.'

'Thank you, I appreciate it,' Sandy replied humbly. 'You're sure talented, by God. Good luck to you, son. Good luck to you.'

Archie stuck out a gnarled and callused hand which Sandy shook. 'My pleasure entirely.'

Archie sniffed. 'I'd better get back tae the bar. They're linin' them up for me.'

'We'll be carryin' you home the night, Archie,' Mick laughed.

Archie winked. 'I hope so. I certainly hope so. It's no every day you retire.'

'What will you do now?' Sandy inquired.

'Sweet fuck all, if I have my way. Sweet fuck all, and enjoy every moment of it.'

Mick was sombre after Archie had left them. 'By the end of next week he'll be wishing he was back at work again,' Mick prophesied. 'I've seen it before. They spend years looking forward to retirement then when it comes it's a complete let down. They wander the streets not knowin' what tae dae wi' themsells. Lost souls. I'm guessin' mind, but Archie probably started when he was twelve and knows nothing else.'

'Maybe he's got a hobby?' Sandy suggested.

Mick shook his head. 'I doubt it! If he's got one at all it's coming in here. Well, he'll have plenty of chance to do that in future, only he won't have the money to indulge hissell. No, not on what he'll have in his pocket from now on in.'

Mick raised the glass of whisky Sandy had just bought him. 'I hope I never come to that. If it was up to me I'd die in harness. So help me, God, and I would. Retirement's a curse in my opinion.'

Sandy stared after Archie's retreating back, hoping Mick was wrong in his prediction.

'So what do you make of the wife?' Mick asked, changing the subject.

'Very nice.'

Mick's chest expanded. 'Fell on my feet there. Quite a "looker", eh?'

'Very much so,' Sandy agreed. In a common way, he qualified silently. But yes, Mick was right.

'A real bobby dazzler. Every day I thank my lucky stars that I met her.

Yes, sir, every bloody day.' And with that Mick turned and beamed in Beryl's direction, to where she was chatting to someone at the bar.

The man was obviously besotted, Sandy realised. He wondered if Mick had any idea of what Beryl had implied she got up to behind his back. He hoped not.

It was growing very hot and stuffy in the pub, Sandy reflected, which was only to be expected with the number of people present. The bar was doing a roaring trade.

Beryl rejoined them a few minutes later to light up yet another cigarette. She took a quick swig of gin before smiling broadly at Sandy. 'I really am impressed. That drawing's the bee's knees. Mick wasn't exaggerating when he said it was good.'

'Thank you,' Sandy acknowledged, feeling uncomfortable at the intense scrutiny from her green eyes. He decided he was going to get out of there as soon as was politely possible. Beryl was definitely trouble, with a capital T.

'Tell us more about yersell. I'm interested,' Beryl prompted.

'Ach, leave the lad alone. I'm sure the last thing he wants is to give us his history,' Mick admonished.

'No, no, that's all right,' Sandy assured him.

He hadn't been speaking for long, Beryl listening in rapt attention, never taking her eyes off him, when Bob came over to the table.

'The collection's been taken and there you are,' he announced, placing a sheaf of notes in front of Sandy. 'I changed it up for you, thinking that would best.'

Here it was, his payment for the drawing. Sandy lifted the sheaf and counted it. 'Eighteen quid!' he gasped in amazement.

'And worth every penny,' Bob nodded. 'There isn't a single person in the pub doesn't think you haven't done a grand job.'

This was far more than Sandy had expected. A fiver at most, he'd thought, and that would have been generous. But eighteen quid! It was unbelievable.

'Thank you,' Sandy spluttered, quite overcome. What a wonderful first commission! And only a drawing too. He couldn't have been more delighted.

'You're welcome. And I hope you'll spend some of it over the bar before you go,' Bob joked.

Sandy, staring at the notes, was in a daze.

* * *

Laura woke with a start. What was that? Something had roused her from sleep. Moments later she heard a sort of retching sound coming from somewhere close by.

There it was again. Someone was ... being sick, she realised. Quickly she slid out of bed, switched on the bedside lamp, and reached for her dressing gown.

She found Sandy in the lavatory with his head in the bowl, vomiting noisily. The stench made her stomach contract.

She knelt beside him. The reason for his condition was obvious, for he stank of alcohol.

'Christ,' he slurred. 'I'm pissed as a newt.'

'Try to be quieter,' she urged. 'You don't want Ma or Pa getting up. They'd go through the roof.'

His head was spinning wildly, while his insides were ... He vomited yet again. Strangely, all he could smell was Beryl's cheap scent.

There was vomit on the outside of the bowl as well, Laura observed. And a splash on the linoleum. She'd clear it up after she got him into bed.

'Feel terrible,' Sandy groaned.

'I'm not surprised. Look at the state you're in.'

'They paid me eighteen quid for the drawing, Laura. Eighteen quid! Can you imagine?'

'That's a lot of money,' she agreed.

She grabbed a hand towel and gave it to him. 'Here. Wipe your mouth if you're finished.'

Was he? He didn't know. He wiped his mouth anyway.

'How did you get home?'

'Taxi.'

'I'm surprised they picked you up like this.'

'I wasn't so bad then ...' He broke off and gulped in air. 'My head's just going round and round.' He took another deep breath. 'It was during the ride I began to feel ill. The night air, I suppose.'

'How much did you drink?'

'Too much,' he groaned.

She studied him grimly. 'Are you going to be sick again?' He considered that. 'I don't think so.'

'Then let's get you through to bed.'

With her assisting him he came unsteadily to his feet where he swayed.

'Lean on me,' she instructed.

He had to, he'd have fallen over otherwise. 'Sorry, Laura. Truly I am.'

'You're the one who'll be sorry in the morning.'

'I think I'll probably die before then.'

That brought a smile to her face. 'I doubt it. But from what little I know of hangovers you're going to have an awfully sore head.'

He moaned in agreement.

'Let's go, one foot in front of the other. And keep it quiet.'

It wasn't easy, even for such a short journey, and at one point she thought, despite her holding him, that he'd still collapse. But eventually she got him into his bedroom and sitting on the bed.

Kneeling, she began undoing his shoelaces. She was just pulling his second shoe off when he, still upright, closed his eyes and started snoring. Ever so slowly, he toppled onto his side.

Laura wondered about taking his trousers off to make it more comfortable for him, then blushed when she realised what she was considering.

It would give her the chance to take a peek at his willy, she thought, blushing even more. It might be the only opportunity she'd get before her wedding night, whenever that might be. She was dying to see what one actually looked like in the flesh and to touch it.

She couldn't, simply couldn't. What if Sandy woke up while she was doing it? And, worse still, remembered in the morning?

Fat chance of that, she thought. He was out cold. But still she couldn't bring herself to do it. He was her brother after all.

After a bit of heaving and manipulating she managed to get his quilt out from under him. When she finally left the room he was nicely tucked up.

* * *

'The morning mail, sir,' Morag announced, presenting a silver salver to Mathew who'd just sat down to breakfast.

'Thank you.'

He flicked through the various items, pausing when he came to one postmarked Canada. 'For you, dear,' he declared, handing an envelope to

Harriet. 'From your sister, it would appear.'

Harriet's face lit up. 'I haven't heard from Cakey in ages. How lovely!'

Mathew frowned. 'I wish you wouldn't refer to her by that ridiculous nickname. She was christened Margaret.'

Harriet laughed. 'She'll always be Cakey to me.'

Laura, toying with some scrambled egg, knew the story of how her Aunt Margaret had come to be called Cakey. It seemed that as an older child she'd been forever in the kitchen baking all manner of cakes, which she simply adored doing. It was her grandparents' cook who'd given her the nickname that had stuck down through the years. She'd met Aunt Cakey only once, a long time ago when she was little. Cakey had been married to a man called Herbert who was now dead. She knew her father had disapproved of Uncle Herbert, considering him to be a 'shady character'. When Uncle Herbert had passed on, from pneumonia, he'd left Aunt Cakey a very rich woman indeed.

Harriet had opened the envelope and begun to read. 'Oh my!' she exclaimed. 'Cakey is coming to visit.'

Mathews fork stopped halfway to his mouth. 'You mean here?'

'Of course, silly. Next month. Isn't that wonderful?'

'Can we have a fresh pot of tea, Morag,' Mathew suddenly snapped. 'This lot is cold.'

'Sorry, sir. Right away, sir.'

Morag collected the offending pot and scurried away.

'And where is Alexander?' Mathew went on in the same bad-tempered tone. 'He should be down by now.'

'Yes, he is rather late,' Harriet agreed without glancing up from her letter.

'I suppose Margaret wants to stay with us?' Mathew queried.

'Well, naturally, dear. I wouldn't expect my sister to book into an hotel. We have plenty of room after all.'

Mathew snorted. That would cause disruption round the house which he hated. He was a very orderly man and loathed being put out in any way, which this impending visit was bound to do.

'Cakey says she plans several excursions round the country,' Harriet informed him. 'And definitely a trip to London for some shopping.'

'Nothing wrong with the shops in Glasgow,' Mathew protested. 'There's no need for her to go to London. She can get anything she might want right here on our doorstep.'

Harriet smiled, thinking how little he knew about women. There was all the difference in the world between Sauchiehall Street and Bond Street. At least so she believed. She had never been to the latter, and knew it by reputation only.

Mathew felt his entire day had been spoiled. He had nothing personally against Margaret, except the man she'd married, of course, but he could have done without her descending on them like this. 'Where is that damned boy?' he grumbled.

'Shall I go and see what's keeping him?' Laura offered, only too aware of the reason why he hadn't appeared for breakfast. 'I've finished anyway.'

'You've hardly eaten a thing,' Harriet protested.

'I've had enough, Ma. Honestly.'

'On you go then.'

'And give Morag a shout,' Mathew added waspishly. 'Tell her to hurry with that tea.'

Laura excused herself and left the room, bumping into Morag outside in the hall. 'Pa's in a right old mood this morning,' she whispered to the maid, who rolled her eyes heavenwards before continuing on her way.

Upstairs Laura halted outside Sandy's bedroom and listened. No snoring, nothing. She tapped. 'Sandy, are you awake?'

There was no reply.

She tapped again, this time louder. 'Sandy?' Again no reply.

Opening the door, she peeked in. Sandy was lying curled in a semicircle, eyes firmly closed. Crossing to him she shook his shoulder. 'Sandy?'

'Sod off,' he rasped.

'It's breakfast time and Pa's asking for you.'

'Can't get up. Can't even open my eyes. Make an excuse for me, Laura, please?' he pleaded.

She stroked his forehead, her fingers coming away covered in sweat. 'I'll try.'

'Thanks.'

On returning to her parents she reported that Sandy had been up to the early hours studying and now wanted a lie-in as a result. Surprisingly, Mathew not only believed her but was actually pleased Sandy was being so diligent with his work.

It was well after noon before Sandy did surface, by which time both his parents were out and not there to see his ashen pallor and pink-tinged eyes.

He couldn't have been more grateful to Laura for covering for him. He was beginning to appreciate his young sister.

Chapter 5

Sandy was sitting at his desk engrossed in working out the odds he was prepared to give for that weekend's horse and dog racing. Every few minutes he consulted one of the various sporting journals and papers he was surrounded by.

It always amazed him how good he was at this, and how profitable a business it was. Or usually was. There were the occasional times when he made a loss but, thankfully, they were few and far between.

He smiled, thinking of the lads at medical school who were his customers, most with more money than sense. Idiots, he thought of them as. Total idiots.

Sighing, he sat back in his chair, allowing himself a brief break. When he'd finished this he'd have to get his head down and study, the exams being only a couple of weeks away.

He was dreading them, absolutely dreading them, and just knew he was going to do badly. If only he had more of an interest in medicine it might have been different, but he didn't and that's all there was to it. The whole thing left him cold.

His gaze strayed over to where his whisky was hidden and he was tempted to have a quick dram. Later, he promised himself. Later. It was far too early to indulge when he had so much to do.

He wondered what Laura was up to? Sitting downstairs with Ma no doubt, Pa having been called out earlier.

He'd have enjoyed her knocking on his door and asking if she could come in for a chat. It was surprising how close they'd become of late, and a revelation on his part the excellent company she could be.

Didn't she have a birthday coming up? For the life of him he couldn't remember the date, but was certain it was soon. He must ask Ma so he could get her a card. Present too, a first on his part. Something nice, but not too expensive or his parents might wonder where he'd got the money from to buy it.

And then he knew what he'd give her. Something she'd already asked for and which he'd refused. He'd draw her and have it framed.

He recalled his argument for refusing her in the first place and it still held true. Nonetheless, that's what he'd do.

He bent again to his task, a pleasure compared to the studying afterwards.

That was tedious in the extreme.

* * *

'Where the hell have you been?' Grant Bell demanded, as Sandy entered the downstairs bar at The Clachan. 'Haven't seen you in ages, me old china.' China was short for china plate, rhyming slang for mate.

'I've been busy. Got the exams coming up,' Sandy replied. He didn't see any reason to explain about Betty's Bar where he'd been doing his recent drinking and which he'd decided to give a miss for a while because of Beryl Gallagher.

'Oh!' Grant nodded, understanding that.

'But I need a night off. All work and no play et cetera, et cetera.'

Grant grinned. 'You can say that again.' He glanced around. 'No talent to speak of here yet. Still, there's plenty of time.'

Women, always women with Grant, Sandy thought. And no success with any of them.

'Martin Benson's about somewhere,' Grant went on. 'Must be in the cludge.' The latter was a Glaswegian word for toilet.

'How's he?'

'Fine. As far as I know. Haven't spoken to him tonight yet. He's with some of his pals from Art School.'

158

Myrtle was busy but Sandy managed to get the attention of another barmaid, one he'd never seen before, and placed his order.

'God, she's ugly,' Grant whispered, nodding in the direction of the new barmaid. 'Got a face like a pissed-on cabbage.'

Sandy couldn't even begin to imagine what a pissed-on cabbage looked like. Still, it was a descriptive phrase.

'So how have you been?' Sandy queried, making small talk.

Grant shrugged. 'The same. Just chugging along.'

Martin Benson came strolling over clutching an empty pint pot. 'Hello, lads.'

'Hello,' Grant replied. Sandy nodded.

'What are you doing tonight?'

'What does it look like?' Grant retorted, his idea of humourous repartee. 'Drinking here, what else?'

Martin winked. 'Fancy coming to a dance? Should be lots of talent there.'

Grant was suddenly very interested. 'A dance where?'

'At the Art School.'

'You're going then?' Sandy queried.

'Oh aye. Wouldn't miss it. But not till later, I want to get a few bevvies down me first.'

'Are you on for it?' Grant asked Sandy.

Sandy wasn't at all sure. It was one thing mingling with art students, another actually going into the Art School itself. He had been in it once before, out of sheer curiosity, but the visit had upset him because he so desperately wished to be attending there rather than where he was. He could remember the feeling, mainly jealousy, quite clearly.

'I don't know,' he prevaricated.

'Oh, come on,' Grant urged. 'As Martin says, there'll be plenty of talent there. It's bound to be a laugh if nothing else.'

For you maybe, Sandy thought sourly. 'Is that French woman ...' He pretended to mentally search for her name. 'Sophie, wasn't it? Will she be there?'

Martin shook his head. 'No idea. She might be. It's possible.'

'You took a right fancy to her, didn't you?' Grant teased.

'Didn't you?'

'True,' Grant admitted. 'I did that.'

'Anyway, you don't have to make up your minds right now. I'll give you the nod when I'm off and you can come, or stay here, as you please,' Martin said.

Sandy had a sip of his pint, and speculated about talking to and dancing with the delectable Sophie. He knew then, despite his misgivings about the place, that he'd give in to temptation and go.

If she wasn't there he could always leave straightaway.

* * *

Sandy recognised many of the faces from The Clachan as students who drank there, but there were many more he didn't.

'Holy shit, just look at some of those birds!' Grant swore softly. 'I think I must have died and gone to Paradise.'

Sandy smiled, there certainly were a lot of good-looking women present, some of them dressed outlandishly to say the least. There again, they were art students, he reminded himself, a breed that liked to be different.

The band, in evening wear, were playing a slow number and the dance floor was packed. Sandy looked around for Sophie, but failed to spot her. Which didn't mean anything, she could still be there somewhere, out of sight for the moment.

'Here goes,' declared Grant, and headed in the direction of a group of women standing talking amongst themselves. The one he chose to ask up, from what Sandy could see anyway, was the least pretty of the lot.

He moved around a bit, edging through the crowd, trying to spot Sophie, but to no avail. Then, all of a sudden, there she was on the dance floor, laughing at something her male companion had obviously just said.

Handsome bugger, Sandy thought morosely. As for Sophie herself, his memory hadn't deceived him, she truly was sensational. A real knock out.

The dress Sophie had on was a shimmering black creation of all silk Charmeuse. It had a scoop neckline, mandarin sleeves and was heavily beaded, in a combination of black and pearl, both front and back. It was finished off with a matching tie round the waist that fell to her knees. Her hair was fastened in a French pleat, quite distinctive from any of the hairstyles of the other women present.

Sandy gnawed a thumbnail as he watched her glide gracefully round the floor, the very epitome of femininity, he thought. In his opinion there wasn't another woman at the dance who could hold a candle to her.

That particular number came to an end and those who'd been dancing applauded politely. Sophie took her partner by the arm and together they walked off.

'Damn!' Sandy swore. She was here with someone. At least so it would seem. All he could do was hang on and see if that really was the case.

He lost sight of her, as she and her dancing partner disappeared into the throng. 'Any luck?'

Sandy turned to find Grant beside him. 'She's here, but with someone, I think.'

Grant pulled a face. 'Too bad.'

'How did you get on?'

'Nice lassie, but she wouldn't stay up. Pity that.' Grant glanced around.

'I don't know what I expected of an Art School dance, but not this. It's all so very ordinary somehow. I'd have thought it would have been a bit more ... well, lively.'

Sandy agreed with that. 'Me too.'

'The lassie was telling me that a lot of these birds aren't students here either, a lot of them are just ordinary working girls simply here for the dance. Surprised me that.'

It surprised Sandy also.

'Well, here I go again,' Grant declared, and strode smartly away. This time it was a red-haired girl he asked up.

Sandy started in the direction of where Sophie had left the floor when suddenly she reappeared with a different chap. The band struck up again and the man took Sophie into his arms.

And so it proved for the rest of the night, Sophie no sooner coming off than she was asked up by someone else. Sandy did everything he could but was thwarted at every turn. No matter where he positioned himself he was never in the right place, and when he finally did get there it was already too late.

Then she came off and disappeared altogether, Sandy unable to find or spot her anywhere. Eventually, thoroughly dejected, he came to the conclusion she'd left.

'Have you managed to get her up yet?'

It was Grant without anyone in tow. Sandy shook his head. 'I think she's gone.'

'Tough luck.'

'And how about you?'

'I'm beginning to get a complex. Is there something wrong with me, Sandy. Something I don't know about?'

That made Sandy smile. 'Not that I'm aware of.'

'I've had eight lassies up, a couple of them crackers, and not one was interested enough to stay and have a second dance.' He shook his head in bewilderment. 'Maybe I say all the wrong things.'

'Maybe.'

'I don't have bad breath, do I?' he asked anxiously.

Sandy laughed. 'Not at all. A bit beery perhaps, but not bad.'

'Well, it isn't that then.'

Sandy made up his mind. 'I'm going home. I've had enough.'

'Have you danced at all?'

'No, I just didn't fancy it.'

'Unless with the French bird, eh?'

Sandy clapped Grant on the shoulder. 'You're hanging on, I presume?'

'Oh aye. Try, try and try again, that's my motto.'

'Then get to it.'

Sandy made his way from the hall, stopping at an open-doored sideroom where a great many drawings and paintings of all sizes were hanging on the walls. The room's lights were on. Curious, he stepped inside.

It was obviously an exhibition of the students' work, each picture having a small card with the artist's name on it pinned beneath. Fascinated, Sandy slowly made his way round the room.

Some of them were terribly good, others not so. At least not in his opinion. He stopped abruptly when he came to an oil of a nude woman whose face was partially turned away from the viewer. He had no trouble recognising Sophie.

What a body, he marvelled in total admiration. Full breasted, a little bulge of tummy, and gently rounded hips that brought his heart into his mouth.

God, you're beautiful, he thought. Absolutely beautiful. He stood, gaze riveted to her naked form, amazed that such a creature should exist. He'd thought her wonderfully good looking fully clothed, but like this, naked ... Words failed him.

He peered at the card beneath the oil which bore the name B. Tanner. Whoever B. Tanner was, he'd done Sophie proud. He was also one lucky bastard to have such a subject to paint.

Eventually Sandy roused himself from his reverie. He couldn't stay here all night, though he might have done if he'd been allowed to.

He had one last look at the painting from the doorway, then headed on down the corridor towards the main entrance. In his mind's eye he was still seeing Sophie in all her glory, quite bedazzled by it.

He decided to walk home as it wasn't that far away, and it was a lovely night, with a myriad stars gracing the heavens.

Sandy had hardly gone any distance at all when he was halted by the sounds of a scuffle along the lane he was passing. Two figures, a man and woman, were struggling, the woman appearing to be trying to beat the man off.

'M'sieur, stop! Stop it!'

The accent was unmistakably French, the word m'sieur a giveaway anyway. Sandy knew beyond the shadow of a doubt, albeit the lane was dark and unlit, that the woman was Sophie.

He didn't consider himself a particularly brave or courageous person, but he didn't hesitate. He ran towards the struggling couple and, reaching them, grabbed the man by his jacket collar and pulled him off.

'What the fuck do you think you're doing?' the young man spat, balling a hand into a fist.

'Are you all right, Sophie?' Sandy demanded, for that's indeed who it was.

'He's drunk,' she replied, voice quivering.

'I think you'd better hop it, pal,' Sandy said to the young man who was glaring at him, adding with a bravado he didn't quite feel, 'while you have the chance.'

If the young man had been about to lash out he now changed his mind. 'Fuck you! Whoever you are.'

Sandy didn't reply to that, as he continued to stand his ground.

Swearing again, the young man abruptly turned and hurried off. 'She's nothing but a bloody French whore anyway!' he shouted back over his shoulder.

'I asked, are you all right?' Sandy queried again.

Sophie's chest was heaving. 'I am. But thank God you came along when you did.'

Her English was good, Sandy thought. He glanced in the direction the young man had taken, then gestured the opposite way. 'I'll walk you down to the street where there are lights,' he offered.

'Thank you.'

They fell into step together, and Sandy noted that she was almost as tall as he. 'I hope he hasn't ruined your dress,' Sandy said. 'It's a lovely one.'

She stopped and stared at him. 'How do you know that? And how do you know my name?'

He laughed, more a release of tension than anything else. 'I was at the dance.'

'Oh! But that still doesn't explain how you know my name.'

'You came into a pub I was in once and the person I was with told me. He's one of the art students.'

She glanced sideways at him. 'You're not. At least, I've never seen you there.'

'I'm studying medicine myself.'

'Ah! You want to be a doctor. A physician?'

'That's the idea.'

He could smell her in the darkness, a rich, warm intoxicating fragrance. Whatever her perfume was, it suited her. Presumably something French. And there was certainly nothing cheap or vulgar about it like Beryl's.

When they reached the main road Sophie immediately opened her coat and examined her dress in the light from the streetlamp.

'Is it torn?'

'No,' she replied in a relieved voice. 'Good. It is pretty.' She smiled at him. 'You're very kind.'

'Not at all.'

She reached up and touched her hair which had become partially undone. 'Merde!' she swore. 'I can't fix it here without a mirror.'

Her make-up was smudged, but Sandy decided not to tell her that as it might only upset her further. 'How on earth did you come to be up a dark lane with that chap anyway?' he queried instead.

She shrugged. 'He's one of the students. When I was leaving the dance he offered to escort me home so that I didn't come to any harm. He told me the lane was a ...' She frowned as she searched her memory. 'How you say, short cut?'

Sandy nodded.

'That would save time. It never crossed my mind he might try and do what he did. He's always seemed such a quiet and polite young man.'

'Well, you're safe now, so may I walk you home instead?' Adding quickly, 'And I promise not to do anything untoward. My word of honour.'

Sophie realised she was more shaken than she'd thought. 'That would be nice ...?' She trailed off and raised an eyebrow, the unspoken question obvious.

'Sandy. Sandy McLean.'

'That would be nice, Sandy.'

'Where do you live?'

He knew the street. It was about ten minutes from there. 'Shall we then?'

His stomach turned over when she slipped an arm through his.

'You're very gallant. A gentleman,' she said as they set off. The compliment thrilled him.

* * *

'Here we are,' she announced.

The tenement was old and run down. One of the windows on the ground floor was boarded up from inside with planks, the glass in front of them broken. Sandy thought the whole street looked hideous and was appalled she lived there.

He looked up at the four storeys, knowing there would be three apartments, or houses as Glaswegians referred to them, on every floor. 'Which one are you?' he asked.

'The top middle.'

He nodded, trying to think of something else to say, not wanting to let her go.

'Thank you again, Sandy. I appreciate what you did.'

He found himself flushing slightly and hoped she didn't notice. 'It was nothing,' he declared modestly.

'Well, I thought it was.' She sighed. 'I must leave you now.'

Come on, he urged himself. Ask her out. Now's your chance, the

opportunity you've been waiting for!
'I was wondering ...' he began slowly.
What gorgeous green eyes she had,
he thought. He ached with the wish
to paint them. Them, and her. He
swallowed hard. 'If you'd care to go
out with me one evening? The
pictures perhaps, or a drink. Or
both?'

She dropped her gaze. 'I'm afraid
not,' she replied in a small voice.

He couldn't have been more
disappointed. 'I see.'

'No you don't.'

'Of course I do. What do you know
about me after all? Nothing, apart
from my name being Sandy McLean
and the fact I'm a medical student.'

'I know enough,' she whispered. 'If things were different, then yes, I would go out with you. But I can't.'

The penny dropped. 'There's someone else?'

Sophie shook her head. 'Not now. But there was until recently. I still ... have feelings for him. It wouldn't be fair to go out with anyone else. Not fair on them you understand.'

'How long since you split?'

'You mean parted?'

Sandy nodded.

'Only a few weeks.'

'And you're still in love with him?'

'Yes,' she whispered. 'I'm so sorry.'

Not as much as he was. Not by a long chalk. 'I can't make you change your mind?'

'No.'

That was it then. 'In which case I'd better be off,' he said reluctantly, but that was the last thing he wanted to do.

'Goodbye, Sandy. Au revoir.'

'Au revoir.'

Her hand fluttered up to his cheek and briefly touched it. Wheeling round she walked into the dimly lit close mouth, the communal entranceway to the tenement, and rapidly vanished upstairs.

Hands in pockets, Sandy trudged back along the street. If the pubs had still been open he'd have gone into one and got roaring drunk.

Life could be terrible at times, he reflected. Now was one such time.

* * *

Sandy woke with an all-consuming feeling of dread and impending doom. The fatal day had arrived, the start of his exams.

'Christ!' he swore softly, wishing with all his heart he'd put more into his studying, that he'd listened more intently at lectures and in the lab. Wishing all manner of things.

Get up, he told himself. But his legs and torso remained exactly where they were. 'Get up!' he said out loud. And still nothing happened.

Closing his eyes, he groaned, a groan from the very depths of his being. Disaster loomed, he just knew it. He couldn't bear to think how his father would react if he didn't do well. All hell, and then some, would break loose.

He lay where he was for another five minutes before managing to summon up the willpower to pull the bedclothes back and swing his legs over the side.

As he dressed he felt he was doing so in preparation for his own execution.

* * *

'Morning, Alexander!' Mathew beamed when Sandy sidled into the room for breakfast. 'A big day ahead, eh?'

Sandy nodded, thinking he wasn't the least bit hungry but had better eat something. To try and settle his stomach, if nothing else.

Laura shot him a sympathetic smile, well aware of what must be going through his mind.

'A good nights sleep, son?' Harriet inquired anxiously.

'Fine, thank you, Ma.' It hadn't been at all, for he'd continually tossed and turned, drifting in and out of consciousness, worry gnawing his insides like a dog at a bone.

'Just toast please. And tea,' he instructed the hovering Morag.

Mathew frowned. 'Nonsense! Bacon and eggs for you, lad, you can't go skimping on a day like today. That right, Harriet?'

'That's right, dear.'

'Yes, Pa,' Sandy agreed meekly. 'Bacon and eggs then please, Morag.'

'Mushroom, tomato and fried bread as well,' Mathew added to the maid. 'The full shebang.'

The thought of eating all that made Sandy feel decidedly queasy. But what could he do? As always, Pa had to be obeyed.

'I remember my exams,' Mathew reminisced, dabbing the corners of his mouth with a napkin. 'One poor chap, can't remember his name now, looked at the paper on the first day, fourth-year exams I seem to recall, and keeled over in a dead faint. Was ever so funny.'

Except for the chap in question, Sandy thought. Poor bugger. He just prayed that didn't happen to him. What a humiliation that would be.

He thanked Morag when she brought him a fresh pot of tea, telling her he'd pour it himself. A mistake he soon realised when his hand shook. Thankfully no one seemed to notice.

'Right!' declared Mathew, rising from the table. 'Must get on. Lots to do.' He glanced at Sandy and smiled. 'Good luck, son, though I doubt you'll need it. You'll sail through your exams, I'm sure.'

'I'll do my best, Pa.'

'That's the stuff to give the troops. Right, Harriet?'

'Right, Mathew.'

'You can tell me all about it when I get home this evening, Alexander,' he said. 'Yes, Pa.'

'I'll be looking forward to that.' He focused on his wife. 'Are you going out today?'

'Perhaps. I don't know yet.'

'Well, if you do don't spend too much. You do have a tendency in that direction.'

Harriet didn't reply, knowing the accusation to be true.

When Sandy's breakfast arrived he bravely tried to eat it, but couldn't. When his mother wasn't looking he hid the fact by draping his napkin over the remains.